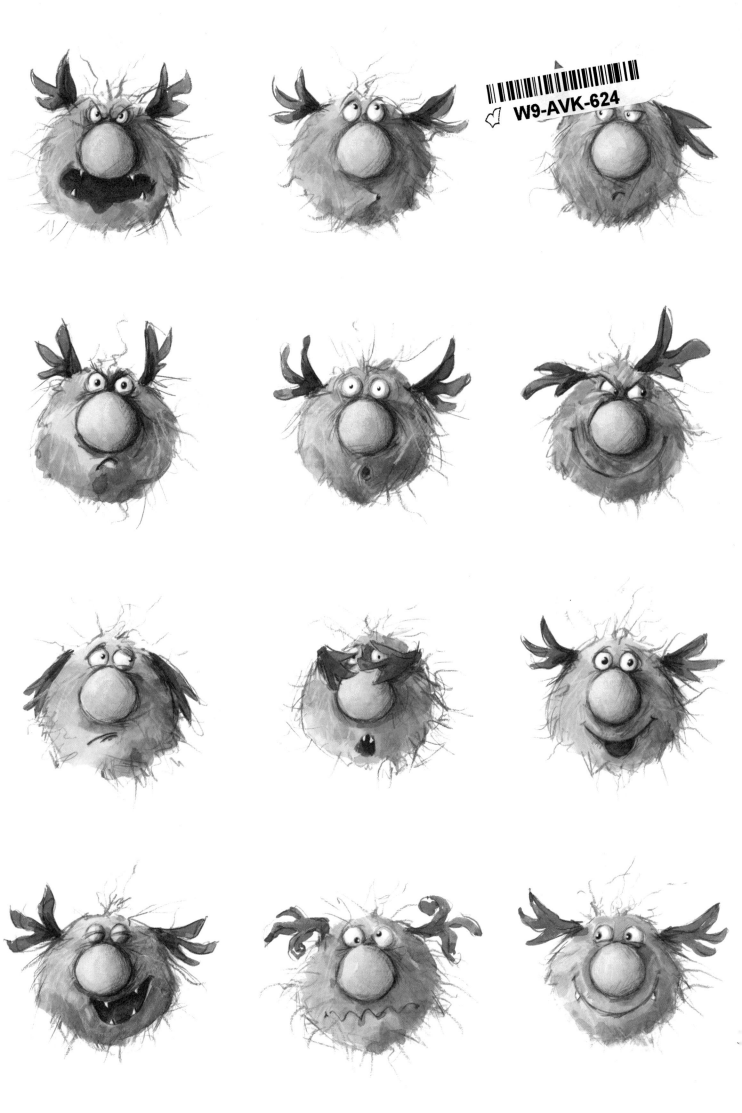

Bine Brändle

FLUSI,
the Sock Monster

First American edition 2004
by Kane/Miller Book Publishers, Inc.
La Jolla, California

Text and illustrations copyright
© 2003 Ravensburger Buchverlag Otto Maier GmbH
First published in Germany in 2003 under the title
"Flusi, das Sockenmonster"

Library of Congress Control Number: 2004100986

Printed in Germany

1 2 3 4 5 6 7 8 9 10

ISBN 1-929132-69-7

FLUSI,
the Sock Monster

Written and illustrated by Bine Brändle

Kane/Miller
BOOK PUBLISHERS

"Oh no! Not again! This is ridiculous! Where are all the socks?" Mum was folding and putting away the laundry.

"Maybe the wind blows them away," suggested Maja. "Or maybe the washing machine gets hungry and eats them." "Maybe," Mum agreed.

Maja looked in her sock drawer
for her favorites.
"Here's one…and…here's the
other one!"
"You're lucky," Mum laughed,
"I don't have a single matching
pair left."

As she pulled on her second sock, Maja felt
something tickle. She wiggled her toes.
"Ouch!" she cried suddenly.
"Something just pinched me!"

Maja pulled off her sock...
...a strange little...*something*...was biting her toe!
"Let go!" cried Maja, and she pulled hard on the
little...*something*...until he finally had to let her go.
"What...What...Who...Who are you?" Maja sputtered.

She glared at him. He glared back.
"Why did you bite me?" Maja finally asked.
The very small...*something*...puffed out his chest
and announced in a very big and very important
voice, "I am FLUSI, the SOCK MONSTER!
Now put me down, or I might have to bite
you again!"

As soon as Maja set him on the ground, he ran right back to her sock and clutched it tightly. "Socks are everything to me!" he cried.

"Sometimes I use a sock for a hat;

sometimes I use a sock to keep warm,

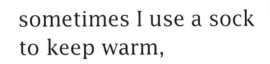

and sometimes I use a sock to hide so no one can see me. (No one is EVER supposed to see me.)

And now, if you promise not to tell," Flusi paused and looked over his shoulder to make sure no one was listening, "I'll show you my favorite place."
"I promise," Maja answered, and together they tiptoed out of her room.

Flusi's favorite place was, of course, the laundry room. He climbed to the top of the washing machine and leapt into the laundry basket. "Yahoo! Swan dive! Watch my back flip!" Again and again he dove into the laundry basket, while Maja clapped and cheered.

"Maja, lunch is ready," Mum suddenly called.
"I'd better go right away before Mum comes looking
for me and discovers you," whispered Maja.
She was barely to the door before Flusi snatched a
clean sock from the basket and disappeared.

Back home in his marvelous sock monster cave, Flusi thought about his new friend Maja. He liked her. (He liked her even though she wasn't supposed to know anything about him.) In fact, he liked her so much that he decided to return the hair clip he'd found a while ago at the bottom of the washing machine.

"Yoo-hoo, Maja, look what I found for you."
Flusi was already in Maja's room when she came back from lunch. Maja bent to give Flusi a big thank-you hug, but Flusi quickly ducked out of her way.
(Sock monsters do NOT hug.)

Maja and Flusi played all day long, stopping only for Maja to have dinner. They played and played and played, right up until bedtime.

Then Maja had what she *thought* was a great idea.
"Here, Flusi, you can sleep in this doll bed. That way
we can be together all day AND all night."
Before Flusi could reply, Maja tucked him into the bed.
"Good night Flusi," she said.
Flusi didn't say anything at all.

As soon as Maja fell asleep he made his escape.
He was furious!
"I am not a stuffed animal! And I'm not going to sleep in
a bed made for a doll!" He ran through the house, back to
his very own marvelous sock monster cave.

The next morning, as soon as she woke up, Maja looked for Flusi. His bed was empty! He was gone! "Oh no! What if Mum found him?"

Even though Mum didn't say anything about Flusi
at breakfast, Maja was still worried. She wasn't
hungry. Nothing tasted very good. All she could
think about was Flusi.

After breakfast, Maja searched the whole house, but she couldn't find Flusi anywhere. If Mum would just leave the laundry room, she could look in there. He must be in his favorite place. But Mum didn't leave. Finally Maja couldn't stand it any longer. She had to look…

"Oh no!"
She'd finally found Flusi.
"Can I help you?" Maja asked Mum suddenly.
"I could rinse the socks for you." Mum looked a
little surprised, but she smiled. "Oh, how sweet
of you, Maja. I'll go make myself a coffee."
The minute Mum was safely out the door, Maja
rescued her waterlogged friend.

"Flusi, I've been looking everywhere for you!
What happened?"
"I was…*blub*…on my way…*blub*…back…*blub, blub*…
to your room, and…"
Flusi's mouth was still a bit soapy.
"… I was…*blub*…trying on a pair of tights I found in
the…*blub*…basket this morning – they would have
made…*blub*…an absolutely terrific coat, by the way –
when suddenly…*blub*…I was grabbed by…*blub*…
two enormous hands…*blub, blub*…

"Flusi, you really need to be more careful."
Maja gently dried her still-dripping friend.
"Why didn't you stay in the doll bed where you
were safe?"
"Because I am NOT a doll OR a stuffed animal!
I am a SOCK MONSTER!"

Flusi climbed slowly down from the counter.
"Flusi, where are you going? Wait a second. Look, I
have a blue sock for you. Wait. Flusi? Flusi?"
But Flusi wasn't interested. Soaking wet and with a
tummy full of soap, he still felt miserable, and
annoyed with Maja and her stupid doll bed.
Without another word he disappeared behind the
washing machine.

"Everyone has a bad day once in a while," Mum told Maja later that night. Maja sighed. If only she could tell Mum how she'd upset Flusi with the doll bed, and how she'd missed him and been so relieved that nothing really bad had happened to him. But she couldn't tell Mum anything about her new friend. She couldn't tell anyone about Flusi. She'd *promised* him. "Things will seem better in the morning," said Mum, and she turned off the light and left the room.

Then, after a minute or two, the door slowly opened. In came a striped sock, moving quickly across the floor. And from under the sock came…

"Oh, Flusi, there you are!" Flusi was happy to see Maja, too. (He would even have given her a hug, if sock monsters did that kind of thing.)

"Thanks for rescuing me this morning,"
Flusi mumbled, not wanting Maja to think he had
completely forgiven her.
"You have to promise me though," Flusi continued,
"that you'll never, ever put me in
a doll bed or with your stuffed animals again.
I am, after all, the SOCK MONSTER!"
Then Maja had what she *knew* was a great idea.

From then on, whenever Flusi felt like a little company, he stayed overnight in his friend Maja's sock drawer, right next to her bed.

So if
sometimes
someone in your house
gets annoyed about missing or disappearing socks,
you might want to be on the lookout for your very
own sock monster. He might be hiding right in
front of your nose – or at least behind your
washing machine!